Harriet Evans

This is
FROG

This is Frog.
Well, actually, this is Tree Frog,
but his friends call him Frog.
Frog lives in the rainforest.

Shall we help Frog jump by
shaking the book up and down?

Frog?

Oh dear...

Quick, let's follow him!
Use your fingers to run up
the page after Frog.

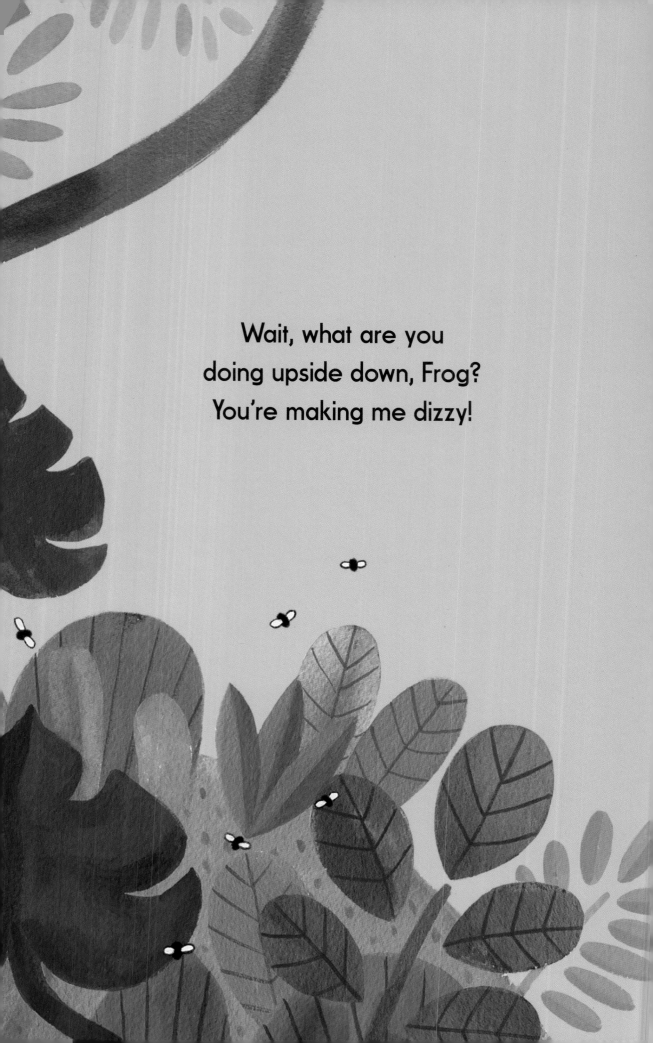

Wait, what are you
doing upside down, Frog?
You're making me dizzy!

Push Frog the right way up onto
the branch with your hand.

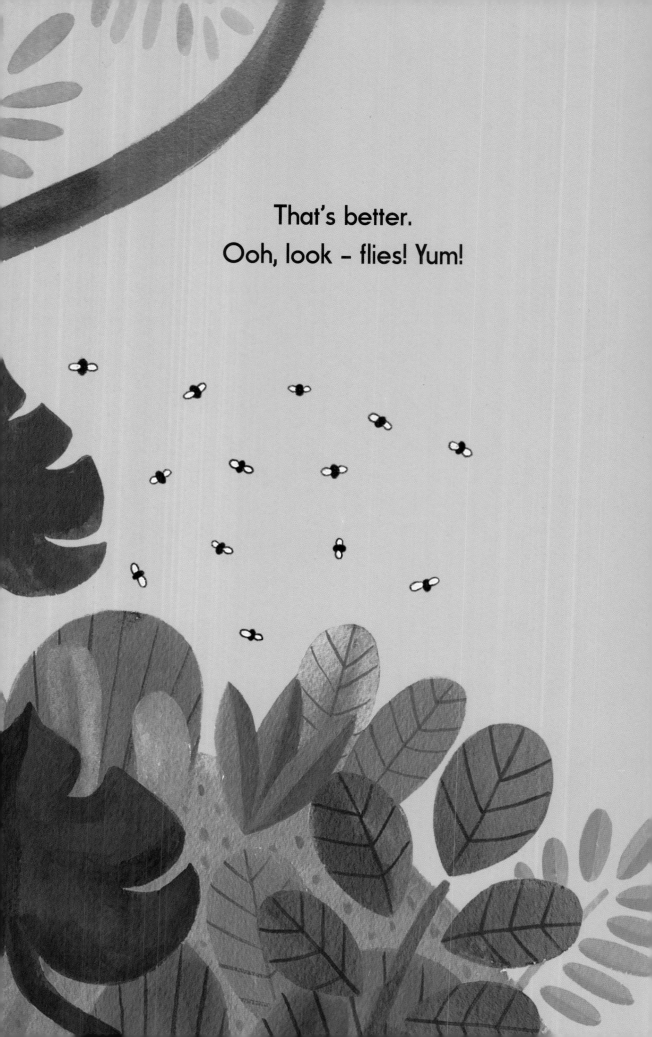

That's better.
Ooh, look – flies! Yum!

Can you blow them towards Frog?

Lots of tasty snacks.

Come on, Frog, you must know what to do now!

What's that, Frog? You've forgotten?
Stick out your tongue to remind Frog.

Well done. Give Frog a cheer!

Mmm, delicious.
The other flies are buzzing off!

Tap them as fast as you can to show
Frog where to find the rest of his meal.

All gobbled up now.
Hey Frog, it looks as if
a friend has come to visit.

Tilt the page to help Frog move closer.

Uh-oh. Maybe not a friend!

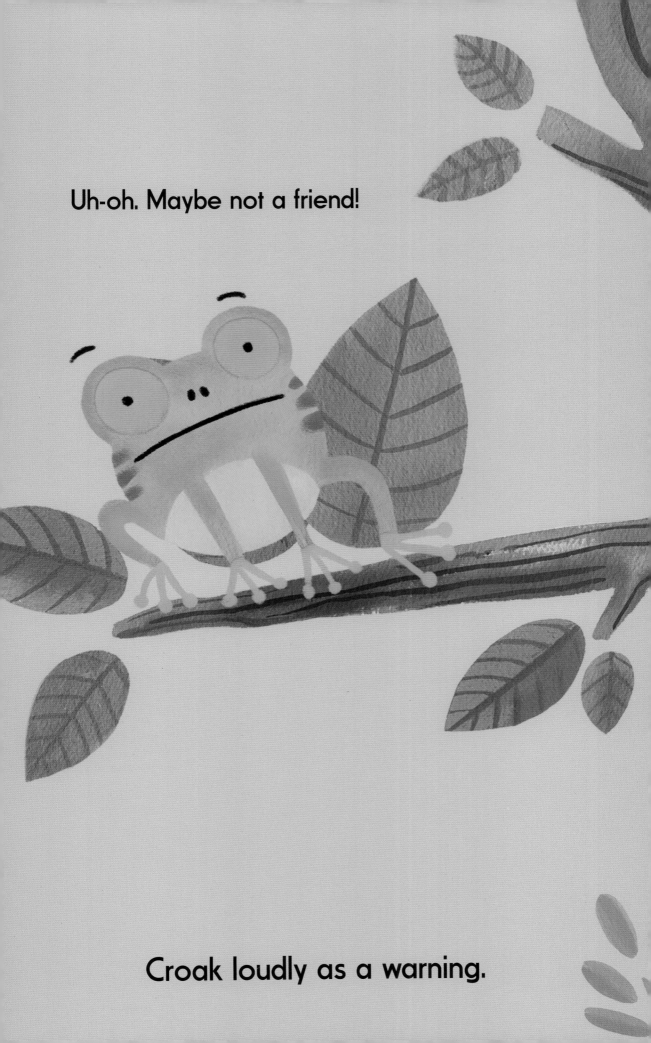

Croak loudly as a warning.

Quick – pull the book
towards you to save Frog!

Phew! That was close.
Frog's still a bit scared.

And another, just in case?

Can you move this leaf over him for camouflage?

Hurray! But wait –
who else is hanging out
on Frog's branch?

Frog is not a big fan
of strangers.

Shake the book to
make them hop off.

Oops! Maybe you shook a bit too hard...

Spin the book all the way
around to help Frog land
the right way up.

Great work! Give yourself a round of applause.

Hang on – is it starting to rain?

Can you count the drops?

Oh no, the rain's getting heavier!

Move the flower over Frog to
shelter him from the monsoon.

Oh sorry, Frog,
I forgot you *like* water!
Let's help him jump
into the pool
below.

Turn the book sideways to prepare for Frog's jump.

Whoa, it's a long way down!

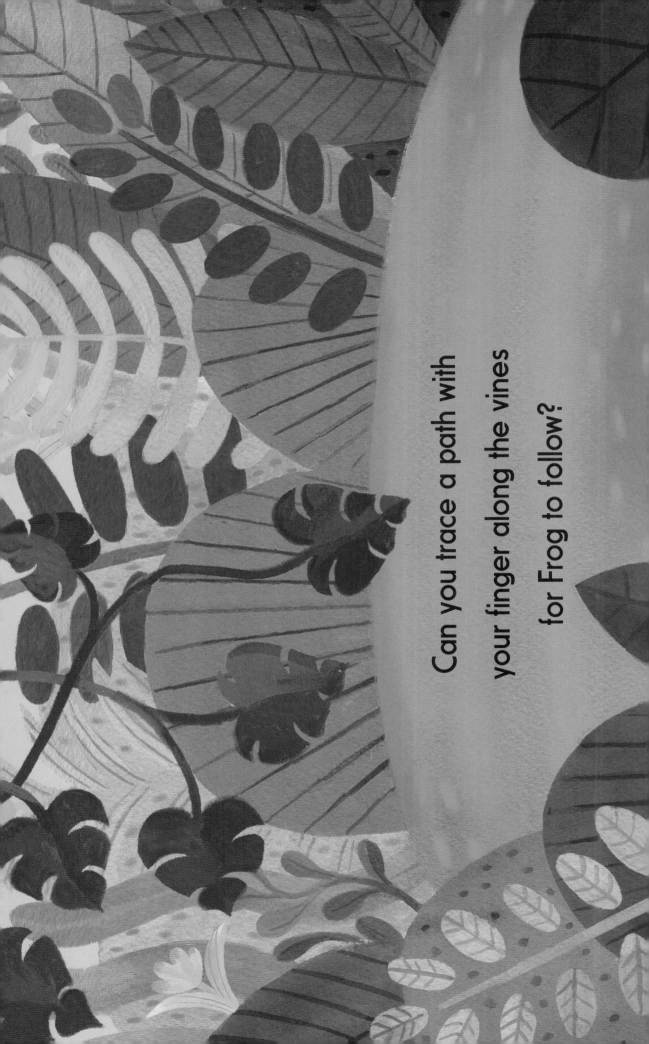

Can you trace a path with
your finger along the vines
for Frog to follow?

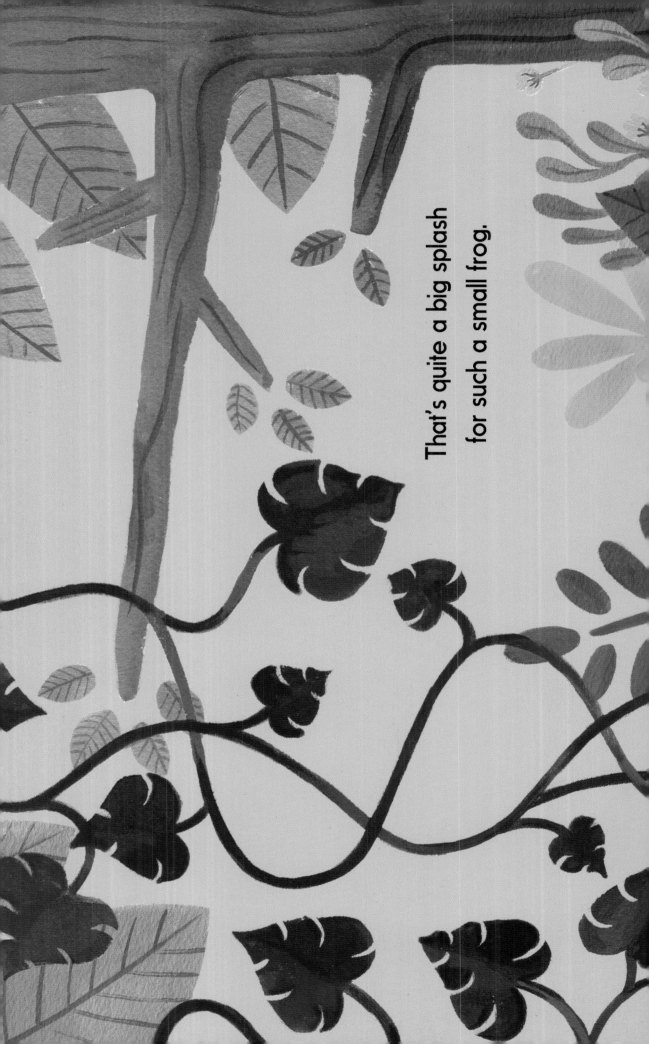

That's quite a big splash
for such a small frog.

Try brushing aside the water so that we can see Frog again.

There you are Frog!

Frog's jump has spun him all over the place. Can you turn the book back?

Flap the pages to help
him swim froggy-paddle.

Okay, that's enough of that.
Frog's a tree frog so he prefers
jumping to swimming.

Can you bounce the book on your knee
to help Frog jump onto the bank?

On dry land again – tree-rific!
Come on Frog, let's hop back
onto your branch.

Frog?